Woman Gored by Bison Lives

Fiction by Douglas Glover

Savage Love (2013)
Bad News of the Heart (2003)
Elle (2003)
16 Categories of Desire (2000)
The Life and Times of Captain N. (1993)
A Guide to Animal Behaviour (1991)
The South Will Rise at Noon (1988)
Dog Attempts to Drown Man in Saskatoon (1985)
Precious (1983)
The Mad River (1981)

DOUGLAS GLOVER

Woman Gored by Bison Lives

GOOSE LANE EDITIONS

"Woman Gored by Bison Lives"
previously appeared in Douglas Glover's
1991 story collection, *A Guide to Animal Behaviour*,
published by Goose Lane Editions.

1

Days, while my husband is at work, Susan and I make love on the couch in her parents' basement. It is a desperate thing to do, and we are both a little stunned by it. But something has pushed us to the edge of caring.

Gabriela, the baby, is upstairs sleeping, while Susan's mother does housework or watches soap operas. We keep our clothes on, manacled at the ankles by a tangle of underwear, jeans, and belts. And when Susan comes, I press my palm across her lips to keep her from shouting out her joy.

I don't know if we are in love. But we are both in need of solace, and our sex is a composition of melancholy and violence, as though we are seeking to escape and punish ourselves in the same act.

The walls are decorated with hangings Susan made during a university art class. The weaving is sinuous and convoluted, with objects embedded or hidden in the loosely spun wool. They are analogues of a spirit that remains secret from me even at the height of passion. Her loom stands idle at the end of the room.

After sex, we lie together on the couch, our tops rucked up so that our breasts crush together, hot and soft, smoking dope and holding slides of Susan's work to the light. I profess to see themes, leitmotifs, and images, and it is true that her work excites me with a mixture of admiration and anxiety (what is hidden; what is lost). But my insights are all superficial, and I cannot connect the woven mysteries with the woman who whispers or the woman who is Gabriela's mother.

Except during sex or when she is crying, Susan's face is expressionless. This is one source of my fascination with her. My own face is endlessly mobile and gives everything away. But Susan is always reserved, watchful, and hidden. At first I took this for a sign of maturity and intelligence. She is tall and graceful, and her silence gives her the appearance of inner poise. I say *appearance*, because it is all a mask. Not even a mask, for the word *mask* implies that it is something she can put on or take off.

Susan's face is forever sad, and her sadness is her strength. Sadness has schooled her in waiting. Her expressionless face conceals her naïveté, her confusion, her lack. She is stunned — that's what her face means. She meets what she cannot understand with a blank stare and a few graceful gestures.

...

A photograph of Susan pregnant — suddenly, I see the significance of the objects hidden in the wall hangings. When I say it, she becomes angry.

Gabriela's father abandoned them before the baby was born. He is a violinist from Toronto. They met when he came to play in the city symphony. How they fell in love, how she became pregnant, seems now unclear in Susan's mind. What is clear is the way they finished. She has told me the story over and over. It is her national epic. It is how her life became the way it is: the baby, her return to Saskatoon and her parents' basement, the idle loom, her job in the composing room at the local newspaper.

The violinist wanted to marry her, she tells me. But his mother interfered. The three of them met — Susan pregnant, expressionless, watchful; the violinist cracking the knuckles of his sinewy, red hands; his mother fierce and excessively thin, calling Susan "my dear girl." The mother said he must not become entangled (like an object in one of Susan's pieces) so early in life or his career would suffer and he would end up mediocre (as she had done). "What she really meant," says Susan, "was that she could not bear to lose him, that he should take a different way." Now he is first violin in another town, his career is mediocre, and he writes wistful letters to Susan and his daughter.

Susan has learned to suffer in silence because there is nothing to say. The violinist and his mother took her voice, and she only dreams of saving enough money to move with Gabriela to a cabin at Pelican Narrows in the north. We make love quietly, secretly, in the long summer afternoons, while the baby sleeps and my husband works at his job at the oil company.

Susan has slept with one other woman. This was in Vancouver in her student days. The woman was her best friend, and they did it once, after a session posing nude for a photography class. "For lust," she says. "In the morning, when we woke up, I couldn't wait to get her out of my bed, out of my house. Do you understand?"

I have red, curly hair, which I wear wild. I dress in faded blue jeans and hiking boots and a worn-out bomber jacket that used to belong to Danny, my husband. I wear three rings in my left ear and a butterfly tattoo above my pubic hair. Susan and I met during Louis Riel Day, when I rode a friend's quarter horse in the annual relay race and came second. She had Gabriela in a backpack and a bandana tied round her head. Her wire-rimmed glasses mirrored the crowds, the dust, the slick wet canoeists, and sweating runners.

We walked along the riverbank together, away from the people (Danny was cooking steaks and burgers for some men's club he belongs to), Susan, quiet, indolent, and graceful (later she confessed her nervousness, how she was so afraid of not making a good impression), and me, hot from the sun and the race. We crossed the railway bridge to the university side and hid among the trees. Susan put the baby down to play and undid her shirt to let the sun touch her breasts. When I kissed her, her eyes widened, her breath quickened. She took my hand and laid it between her breasts.

Danny is a sad man. He knows what's going on — up to a point. He knows I'm bored because he's bored. He doesn't like himself, so he's not surprised that I don't care much either. He plays ball in the summer, hockey in the winter. He's joined the Lions because his father was a Lion. Once a month he drives to the family place in the Qu'Appelle Valley for the weekend to check on his mother and talk to the neighbour who rents her last half-section of land. The old house needs paint and the barn is beginning to collapse.

He loves the place, but he could never earn enough money farming to make a go of it. He doesn't even like farming. He's got a good job publishing an in-house magazine for an oil company, but he's not a company man and hates the work. He dreams of selling up and moving to a cabin in the mountains to write a novel. But every novel he starts is about himself and he gets bored with it after the first four or five paragraphs.

He married me because I was different from the farm girls he knew growing up, those earnest, practical girls in jeans and white blouses. I almost laugh when I think of how he stared and stared at my tattoo. It's amazing what a tattoo will do to counteract the effect of a plain face and red hair. He thought I'd be the spark his novel was missing, the novel of his life. I married him for his bomber jacket. In this way we fall in love with things rather than people. It's only after you're married that you discover the recalcitrant baggage of personality attached to the bright, attractive object.

...

"We're at our best," says Susan, "when we have nothing to lose."

One day we take Gabriela and a picnic and drive north toward Prince Albert. We drink wine from a bottle along the way. The sun glares off the windshield, the wine bottle, and Susan's glasses. She gives Gabriela a sip of wine and removes the little girl's shirt in the back seat.

We drive to Batoche and visit the battle site, then head for a nearby park and hike into the woods. It's a weekday so there is no one around. We take off our clothes and the baby's clothes. We lie together on a blanket with the food and wine around us, the hot sun warming the three of us, the naked baby crawling over our hot bodies.

Susan's cheeks are flushed. When I touch her, she shivers. For a while, we curl up, Susan with her back to me, my hand caressing her hair, her breasts, her sloping belly. Gabriela plays in the leaves. Later I take pictures of the mother and daughter together, then Susan pushes me down on the blanket and kneels between my legs and kisses me.

We get dressed as the afternoon wears on and drive farther to an animal park where there are bison. Susan wants to see them; I want a photograph. There is a herd of cows and calves and one lone bull with a matted hump, but they are too far away for a decent shot. Gabriela and Susan walk a few steps, hand in hand, along the fence, pausing to pull up grass and hold it between the wires. I focus and focus, but nothing satisfies me. I am hot, light-headed from the wine and sun, anxious because all I can think of is the three naked females like goddesses under the hot sun.

It is difficult to describe precise states of mind. My style of abandonment is sentimental and hopeless. Sex is only a variant of nostalgia. I am so unhappy with Danny. I feel a quiver between my legs; I want something from Susan, something no one can give, want only perhaps that the afternoon will go on and on.

All at once Susan turns back to me and points the way we have come. A woman with a tiny Instamatic camera in her hand has crawled clumsily over the fence and is walking across the short grass toward the grazing cows. Her husband and two children stand outside the fence watching. I am looking through the viewfinder; Susan whispers something. I swing and sight the bull. He, too, is watching the woman with the Instamatic. His hooves drag at the earth. Shreds of old wool dangle in dusty hanks from his shoulder hump, like Susan's wall hangings.

I focus on the woman again, asking myself what dream has led her onto the buffalo prairie. A few moments before, we had passed the couple with their children and heard her speak sharp words in a British accent. She is wearing a denim skirt wrapped around her bulging hips, a hooded sweatshirt, pink running shoes, and thick glasses. Her lank hair flaps at her sunburned cheeks like crow wings. Her husband points, drawing the children's attention to their fearless mother.

I begin to shoot film as the bull dips his huge, awkward head and snorts. He trots in the woman's direction. She turns awkwardly and begins to run toward the fence, emitting high-pitched yips of panic, her Instamatic flapping on its wrist-strap. At the moment the bull reaches her, I stop winding the film forward; I shoot and shoot, exposing the same frame over and over.

2

Susan dies. This happens a year after we watch the bison gore the English tourist north of Batoche. She probably had the cancer even then, or so the doctor said. Danny leaves me sometime during that year, I forget when, though he still comes around to sit and visit. He does just sit, saying nothing. He still has nothing to say. But he has this impulse to comfort me with his company. He goes away angry because I can't be comforted, because I am outrageously inconsolable, because I have lost everything, because I just sit there smoking dope, sucking peppermint candies, and crying in a room where the walls are covered with Susan's artwork.

The last one, the piece she did between the time we watched the bison gore the woman and the time Susan died, hangs above my pillow. It's a bag woven of binder twine, frayed burlap, and burst milkweed pods with their parachute seeds trailing down. Mornings I wake with milkweed seeds on my eyelids — usually I have dreamed Susan is kissing me. You can see the contents of the bag through the loose weaving: one of Gabriela's baby shoes, a dried up butterfly, photos of Susan and the baby naked, a plastic laminated newspaper headline. The bag was empty when she finished it; I am the one who placed these relics inside.

...

I develop the photographs from the afternoon at the bison park. I do this the same evening. Susan is as anxious as I am to see once again what we have seen: that lumpish, stupid woman, with her crow-wing hair, trotting toward the buffalo herd. Clearly, what we see in her is what we fear most in ourselves — ugliness and exposure.

But the pictures are a disappointment. The woman is too far away; the pictures are all sky and scrub prairie like the prairie snapshots amateurs take. The frame of multiple exposures shows only a tangled blur of movement, tiny bison legs, like fragments of prehistoric cave paintings, and an arc of white which could be the woman's face or her thighs.

The newspaper the next day tells the story: WOMAN GORED BY BISON LIVES. They are an immigrant family, freshly arrived from Saffron Walden. He is a fireman; she, a housewife. They had never seen bison before, had no idea they weren't as tame as cattle. Climbing that fence, the woman had simply wanted to get a better shot to send to her parents.

The bison's horn had severed an artery in her thigh, a potentially fatal wound — we had seen this and the aftermath: wardens shouting and flagging their arms to shoo the animals away, a man's hand pressed roughly against the wound, the tourniquet band twisted deep into her floury flesh, the husband's pale face as he held both children and looked about in shock.

Susan cuts out the article to keep.

We go to the hospital to visit the woman the bison gored. Her name is Ruth Hawking. We bring her flowers, chocolates (she looks like she eats a lot of chocolate), and magazines (magazines with photographs of thin, glamorous models). We go waltzing in with our gifts and shoo her surprised husband out the door. We say we read about the accident in the paper and thought we would like to cheer her up. Susan has made a special get-well card out of the photographs I took, gluing them together, end to end, in sequence, so that they unfold in an accordion panorama. When the woman sees the photographs, she starts to weep. The message on the card reads: WHAT IS WRONG WITH THIS PICTURE?

This is a cruel thing to do, but we have temporarily lost perspective. Actually, we are in the hospital for Susan's tests. Gabriela is with her grandmother; Danny is at the oil company. Susan and I are stoned. Her glasses keep falling down her nose. Last night I made her swallow five pearls so that the internist would have something good to look at when the X-rays were developed. "One thing," she says, "if this is bad, don't ever let me get un-stoned."

It's bad. Suddenly, all breasts become ominous objects, growths hanging clamped to your chest like limpet mines, getting ready to kill you. Only three pearls come out. We get the X-rays and look for the other two, holding the plastic negatives up to the light in Susan's basement. I'm shocked to see the white ghost bones and the fibre nets of Susan's organs.

She's still healthy, still makes love (later, her breath turns sour, and lumps appear like black pearls beneath her skin), only our love is more violent and perverse. She craves a pain she can enjoy. Her eyes are greedy for it. Perhaps it is some kind of voodoo she makes against the pain that will come later. Or (I never tell her this) perhaps it is only that she hates herself, that she sees herself as already dead, and only the pain can make her feel alive.

She throws her head back, her eyelids slip shut, and she sighs, "Kill me, kill me," meaning "Save me, save me" or "Love me, love me."

...

Susan's real self begins to emerge. At first, as she loses weight, she is more beautiful than I could have imagined. The mask does not drop away, but it becomes more expressive, more complex in its implications (what it hides). She begins to weave again. She sits for hours at her loom with the baby on the bench next to her. She doesn't do this for the sake of art; it's so that Gabriela will retain an image of an industrious, capable mother. Gabriela, of course, has very little to say, but shows a surprising aptitude for entangling herself in whatever Susan is doing.

My obsession with photographing her (during this period, I take hundreds of pictures) seems morbid to Susan, but she puts up with it. I take photographs of all her activities: pictures of Susan cleaning house, sitting on the toilet, shopping, weaving, caring for Gabriela. I do a whole series of photos of Susan sleeping and another of Susan's face during orgasm. I do black-and-white studies of different parts of her body: hands, ear-lobes, nape of neck, nipples.

One day I follow her to work and spend an hour shooting her as she cuts the galleys into columns of print, waxes the paper, and pastes the stories, headlines, and ads onto her layout board. In her hands, the lines of type seem to curve and intersect like the cloth strands of her tapestries.

Secretly, we both know I am making provision for a future she will not share, getting ready for the time when she will be absent. She, too, is getting ready.

Nights, now that her parents understand our situation, I sometimes sleep in her bed. (Nothing was said, only things became, for them, suddenly clear; they have begun to treat me with a certain gentle deference and formality which are tokens of their affection.) In the middle of the night, I'll wake up and watch her breathe. When she stirs, she sees that I am weeping. "I miss you already," I say. "It hurts so much I can hardly stand it." "What's the worst thing?" she asks. "I'm afraid that when you die it will be awful, that you'll choke or vomit and be terrified." She stares at me, saying nothing, and I know I have said the words she would have said herself.

We discuss Gabriela endlessly. Her parents are too elderly to cope alone, Susan thinks. I say I want the baby, that I'll take care of her because of the part of Susan that's in her. Susan says, "Yes." But the next thing I know, she has made up a questionnaire and mailed it to all her relatives and friends. It begins, "I am dying of cancer. Soon my baby will need a new family. You can help me decide what to do about this by filling out and returning the following information sheet."

The things Susan wants to know include: "Do you believe life is a journey or a trial? Am I being punished? What are your thoughts on hope? Has my life been a waste? Will you continue to love and cherish my baby girl even if she is a flop? How many times a day do you feel joy? Have orgasms? What is the reason for men?"

After the forms come back, we make trips to conduct interviews, until Susan finally decides to leave Gabriela with an older sister in Medicine Hat. The sister has twin boys a year older than Gabriela; her husband is an ex-rodeo rider who owns his own air-freight business, which specializes in transporting horses. "I want her to have some men around," says Susan, "the kind of men that'll make up for her father." "What about me?" I ask. "You're her auntie. You'll always be there. You'll keep her from growing up ordinary. When the time comes, you'll tell her everything about me. She'll need to know."

One day (it's winter now) Danny and I take Susan and the baby to the city zoo. Danny is already looking for an apartment; our house is up for sale. Susan insists on carrying Gabriela as we walk among the pens and cages, until she gets tired and hands the baby to my husband. She leans on me as we walk; she's forgotten her mitts, so I give her one of mine, and we walk with our arms around each other, our bare hands buried in one another's coat pocket. To our surprise, Danny's good with Gabriela. He makes her laugh, holds her up to the fences to pet the animals and talks, talks, talks to her, though she never says a word back. "She's in love," says Susan. "She can't take her eyes off him."

We are all sad, feeling that, though we are together, we shall soon be apart for good. No one is angry. The level of disaster that has befallen us makes it seem impossible that any one person could have caused it. Walking through the zoo, we feel the dignity of companions in tragedy. We are not defeated, even though certain things are almost over, almost behind us. There is a sense in which I find this deeply satisfying. This is the way all life should be, I think, wishing only that Susan could go on dying, that my husband could go on leaving me, that we could forever be dispensed from living our humdrum lives — that desert of emotion.

We pause to smoke a joint at the bison pen, where the huge, lumbering beasts stand with their faces to the wind, chewing their hay. Susan and I are reminded of the day we watched the bull gore the woman from Saffron Walden. We have avidly followed Ruth Hawking's subsequent career in the papers — she has been arrested once for shoplifting and twice for reckless driving leading to minor accidents. Susan, always so restrained, gets the giggles whenever she sees these announcements. She says, "That woman the bison gored is *still* alive!"

The zoo bison look ungainly and alien, which they are, left over, as it were, from another time.

The fences, the baled hay, the feeding rick, and the low zoo buildings in the background, all contribute to this sense of dislocation. Except when seen attacking women, they are somewhat boring. They produce in me, for example, only a mild anxiety, a feeling that things aren't right, that there is much to be guilty for.

I look at Danny and say to Susan, "You know, he's not such a bad guy. I haven't been a very good wife to him." Susan starts to laugh. She gets hysterical and has to sit down on the cold ground. My hand is tangled in her coat pocket so that I fall down with her. Our laughter startles the bison, which glance warily in our direction.

Danny comes over with the baby to see what's wrong. Susan tells him what I said, that I haven't been a very good wife. Danny grins. He says, "That's an understatement." "That's what I said," says Susan, snorting with laughter. "Poor bunny," I say. "I'm sorry." He hands me the baby and helps us up. Tenderly, he pulls Susan's coat together at the throat and tucks her scarf in.

She watches. She soaks things up through her eyes. She stares at Gabriela for hours on end, hungrily absorbing every whim and turn of emotion. As she gets closer to the end, everything but the child becomes superfluous. "I don't want to forget her," she says. (What she means by this is a mystery about which I cannot bear to question her.)

About an hour before Susan dies, she opens her eyes and says to me, "Well, here we go." Her lungs begin to fill up, her breathing grows shallower. She makes a horrible bubbling sound in her chest, which I suppose is what they used to mean by the phrase "death rattle." Her mother holds her head. I sit on the bed, clutching Susan's hand.

Soon she is breathing air only into her throat. Then I think she must be dead, but her mouth keeps opening as though she were still breathing. It opens once or twice by reflex. I think this time she must really be dead. But then her chin moves once more and I feel a tremor in her hand. I say, "Go, baby sweetheart. It's okay. I'm here. You can go and not be afraid because we're here with you." Finally, she is dead, though I am not certain when the borderline was crossed, only that she is on the other side. Her mother lets her down and starts, through her tears, to sing a lullaby.

Susan's head is thrown back and slightly to the side, her mouth open. I recognize the pose. I've seen it in old paintings — it is the moment when the soul escapes through the mouth on its way to become a star. That's an outdated mythological reference, I know, a leftover, like the bison. But I haven't got anything else. It just looks like that.

I go to see Ruth Hawking. (Her husband's name is in the new phone book.) This is a little pilgrimage for Susan. But Ruth is gone. She left him with the kids and flew back to Saffron Walden. Her husband, a lonely, harried man, tells me, "She had a difficult time adjusting to life in Canada."

He invites me in, but has nothing more to add, and I leave after a few awkward minutes. ("Men!" I say to myself.)

3

I go to Medicine Hat for a visit. I like the area. All of a sudden, it strikes me that I really want a place of my own just outside of town where the dry chinook winds blow endlessly in the caragana and nothing stops the eye. I take Gabriela for a drive to look at real estate. (I get a list from a broker.)

Communication is now possible, up to a point. We stop at a roadside table to eat our picnic lunch. I take out a ball of yarn and begin to teach her the Cat's Cradle. I don't really know how to make a Cat's Cradle myself, but I have brought a book and there is plenty of yarn. She is a reserved and intelligent child with Susan's eyes. Watching my fingers fumble with the yarn, her face becomes a mask.

I say to her, "There are certain things you have to know. Suicide is not an option. Life is always better under the influence of mild intoxicants. Masturbation is healthy, the sooner started the better. It's a sin not to take love where you find it. That is the only sin. I have photographs of your mother."

photo: Bill Gilduz

DOUGLAS GLOVER's bestselling novel *Elle* won the Governor General's Award for fiction and was a finalist for the International IMPAC Dublin Literary Award. His stories have been frequently anthologized, notably in *The Best American Short Stories*, *Best Canadian Stories*, and *The New Oxford Book of Canadian Stories*. In 2006 Glover was awarded the Writers' Trust of Canada Timothy Findley Award for his body of work. Follow Douglas Glover at the online magazine *Numéro Cinq*, where he is publisher and eminence grise.

Copyright © 1991, 2014 by Douglas Glover.

All rights reserved. No part of this work may be reproduced or used in any form or by any means, electronic or mechanical, including photocopying, recording or any retrieval system, without the prior written permission of the publisher or a licence from the Canadian Copyright Licensing Agency (Access Copyright). To contact Access Copyright, visit www.accesscopyright.ca or call 1-800-893-5777.

Series edited by Martin James Ainsley.
Cover and series design by Chris Tompkins.
Art direction and page design by Julie Scriver.
Printed in Canada.
10 9 8 7 6 5 4 3 2 1

Library and Archives Canada Cataloguing in Publication

    Six@sixty / edited by Martin James Ainsley.

Short stories compiled to commemorate Goose Lane's sixtieth anniversary.
    2. Woman gored by bison lives / Douglas Glover.
Issued in print and electronic formats.
ISBN 978-0-86492-853-5 (set : pbk.).—ISBN 978-0-86492-793-4 (set : epub).—
ISBN 978-0-86492-855-9 (v. 2 : pbk.).—ISBN 978-0-86492-733-0 (v. 2 : epub).

    I. Ainsley, Martin James, 1969-, editor. II. Glover, Douglas, 1948- .
Woman gored by bison lives.

PS8321.S59 2014   C813'.010806   C2014-902978-0
                                                                                                 C2014-903186-6

Goose Lane Editions acknowledges the generous support of the Canada Council for the Arts, the Government of Canada through the Canada Book Fund (CBF), and the Government of New Brunswick through the Department of Tourism, Heritage, and Culture.

Goose Lane Editions
500 Beaverbrook Court, Suite 330
Fredericton, New Brunswick
CANADA E3B 5X4
www.gooselane.com

This book, typeset in Minion Pro
and Gill Sans, was printed and bound in Canada by
Friesens in Altona, Manitoba, on 55 lb. Rolland Enviro
100 FSC Natural Antique.